Mighty Mighty MONSTERS

# THE ABOMINABLE
# Snow Kid

STONE ARCH BOOKS
a capstone imprint

Mighty Mighty Monsters are published by
Stone Arch Books, A Capstone Imprint
1710 Roe Crest Drive
North Mankato, Minnesota 56003
www.capstonepub.com

Library of Congress Cataloging-in-
Publication Data

ISBN: 978-1-4342-3892-4 (library binding)
ISBN: 978-1-4342-4227-3 (paperback)
ISBN: 978-1-4342-4650-9 (eBook)

Summary: Winter has pounced on
Transylmania in full force. While the kids
are thrilled to have a snow day, their good
times are cut short when they realize the
cause: An Abominable Snow Kid has moved
to Transylmania, and she has brought Old
Man Winter along with her!

Printed in the United States of America in
North Mankato, Minnesota.
032013
007223CGF13

Mighty Mighty MONSTERS

# THE ABOMINABLE
## Snow Kid

created by
**Sean O'Reilly**

illustrated by
**Arcana Studio**

In a strange corner of the world known as Transylmania . . .

Legendary monsters were born.

WELCOME TO TRANSYLMANIA

But long before their frightful fame, these classic creatures faced fears of their own.

To take on terrifying teachers and homework horrors,
they formed the most fearsome friendship on Earth . . .

# Mighty Mighty MONSTERS

# MEET THE MONSTERS!

**CLAUDE**
The Invisible Boy

**FRANKIE**
Frankenstein

**MARY**
Future Bride of
Frankenstein

**POTO**
The Phantom
of the Opera

**MILTON**
The Grim Reaper

30

Ellie ran . . .

Vlad, wait!

I know what it's like to be the new girl in town.

I'll go talk to her.

But, Kitsune –

Trust me on this.

I hope she's right.

# ABOUT
# SEAN O'REILLY
## AND ARCANA STUDIO

As a lifelong comics fan, Sean O'Reilly dreamed of becoming a comic book creator. In 2004, he realized that dream by creating Arcana Studio. In one short year, O'Reilly took his studio from a one-person operation in his basement to an award-winning comic book publisher with more than 150 graphic novels produced for Harper Collins, Simon & Schuster, Random House, Scholastic, and others.

Within a year, the company won many awards including the Shuster Award for Outstanding Publisher and the Moonbeam Award for topchildren's graphic novel. O'Reilly also won the Top 40 Under 40 award from the city of Vancouver and authored The Clockwork Girl for Top Graphic Novel at Book Expo America in 2009. Currently, O'Reilly is one of the most prolific independent comic book writers in Canada. While showing no signs of slowing down in comics, he now writes screenplays and adapts his creations for the big screen.

# GLOSSARY

**appropriate** (uh-PROH-pree-uht)—suitable for the situation, or right, as in appropriate attire

**blizzard** (BLIZ-urd)—a heavy snowstorm, often with strong winds

**climate** (KLYE-mit)—the usual weather in a certain place

**curious** (KYUR-ee-uhss)—eager to find something out, or interested in understanding how something works

**honest** (ON-ist)—an honest person is truthful who does not lie or steal or cheat

**officially** (uh-FISH-uhl-ee)—if something is official, it has been approved by someone in authority

**relax** (ri-LAKS)—to calm down, or become less tense and anxious

**tentacles** (TEN-tuh-kuhlz)—one of the long, flexible limbs of some animales like the octopus and squid

# DISCUSSION QUESTIONS

1. Which Mighty Mighty Monster is your favorite? Why? Discuss your favorite monsters.

2. As long as Ellie is in Transylmania, there will never be another spring. If you could have only one season for the rest of your life, which one would you choose? Why?

3. Old Man Winter can travel anywhere in the world instantly. If you could teleport, where would you go? What places would you visit? Talk about traveling.

# WRITING PROMPTS

1. Imagine another new monster has come to Transylmania. Who is he or she? Write about your new monster, and then draw a picture of him or her.

2. The Mighty Mighty Monsters get a snow day. What would you do if school were canceled because of a blizzard? Write about your day off.

3. Even though they're friends, the gang has to tell Ellie to leave. Have you ever told someone you cared about something that wasn't easy to say? Write about it.

# Mighty Mighty MONSTERS ADVENTURES

Mighty Mighty MONSTERS
The KING of HALLOWEEN CASTLE
GRAPHIC NOVEL

Mighty Mighty MONSTERS
HIDE and SHRIEK!
GRAPHIC NOVEL

Mighty Mighty MONSTERS
Lost in SPOOKY FOREST
by Sean O'Reilly
GRAPHIC NOVEL

Mighty Mighty MONSTERS
My MISSING MONSTER
by Sean O'Reilly

Mighty Mighty MONSTERS
NEW MONSTER in SCHOOL
by Sean O'Reilly
GRAPHIC NOVEL

Mighty Mighty MONSTERS
MONSTER MANSION
by Sean O'Reilly
GRAPHIC NOVEL

Mighty Mighty MONSTERS
THE MONSTER CROOKS
by Sean O'Reilly
GRAPHIC NOVEL

# THE FUN DOESN'T STOP HERE!

## DISCOVER MORE:
- VIDEOS & CONTESTS!
- GAMES & PUZZLES!
- HEROES & VILLAINS!
- AUTHORS & ILLUSTRATORS!

# www.capstonekids.com

Find cool websites and more books like this one
at www.facthound.com  Just type in Book I.D.
9781434238924 and you're ready to go!